TEENY HOUDINI

BOOK 2:

THE SUPER-SECRET VALENTINE

The TEENY HOUDINI Series

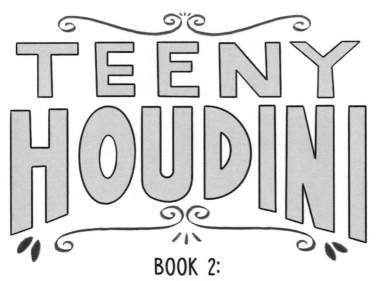

TEENY HOUDINI

BOOK 2:
THE SUPER-SECRET VALENTINE

BY **KATRINA MOORE** ILLUSTRATIONS BY **ZOE SI**

Katherine Tegen Books is an imprint of HarperCollins Publishers.

Teeny Houdini #2: The Super-Secret Valentine
Text copyright © 2022 by Katrina Moore
Illustration copyright © 2022 by Zoe Si
All rights reserved. Printed in the United States of America.
No part of this book may be used or reproduced in any manner whatsoever
without written permission except in the case of brief quotations embodied in critical
articles and reviews. For information address HarperCollins Children's Books,
a division of HarperCollins Publishers, 195 Broadway, New York, NY 10007.
www.harpercollinschildrens.com

Library of Congress Control Number: 2021943907
ISBN 978-0-06-300464-1 (trade bdg.) — ISBN 978-0-06-300465-8 (pbk.)

Typography by Andrea Vandergrift
21 22 23 24 25 PC/LSCC 10 9 8 7 6 5 4 3 2 1

First Edition

1

A Magician's Box

*S*quirt!

I squeeze a big glob of glue onto my Valentine's Day box. Then I pour a million gazillion rainbow sparkles on the glue glob. Ooh-la-laddie! It's so fancy!

It is three days before the big Valentine's Day party. My first-grade class is decorating our Valentine's Day boxes. All the valentines that I get from my classmates will go in this box. My box will be extra magical, just like me!

I am Bessie Lee. Gramma calls me Gah Yee, my Chinese name. Bailey, my ten-year-old sister, calls me annoying. And everyone calls me teeny. Because I *am* teeny. I am the teeniest at the restaurant tables. I am the teeniest at the movie theater. Most of all, I am the teeniest in my class *and* in my family.

Sometimes I call myself Teeny Houdini. That's because I'm magic. Just like the greatest magician of all time, Harry Houdini. I am magic, for real. I made myself disappear at

our fall talent show. Also, I have a magic hat, a magic wand, a special magic cape, and a real bunny, Baby Rabbit. Plus, Gramma gave me a book, *Abracadabra: Magic for Kids*. It's full of magic tricks. Bailey helps me practice them if I beg her enough.

Everyone likes my magic . . . Mom, Daddy, Gramma, Bailey, Baby Rabbit, Ms. Stoltz, and my friend Ella. The only one who doesn't is . . . Margo.

Margo sits right next to me. She always tattles on me. Bailey says my teacher must have a *funny sense of humor* to put me and Margo next to each other in class. I don't think it's funny. Margo and I are opposites. *Opposites* means you are not the same AT ALL!

Right now, Margo's making a heart on her pink Valentine's Day box out of glue. She squeezes itty-bitty dots. *Just one dot at a time.*

Just like Ms. Stoltz said. Margo always follows the rules.

My box has different-colored paper hearts all over it. I cut and glued them all by myself. And then I stuck streamers everywhere. And added shiny stickers.

"Ta-da! A magician's box!" I yell.

Ella comes over to look.

"It's awesome!" she says.

"It just needs one more thing . . . ," I tell her.

But I am out of glue. I look back at Ella's desk to see if she has any left.

"Look at your box, Ella! I love it!" I say.

Ella colored her box turquoise, her favorite color. There are brown puff balls on the top. Each puff ball has a sprinkle of brown sparkles on it. I point to a puff ball.

"Those look like the chocolate snacks your mom packs you," I say.

"Yeah!" Ella says. "My *mamãe* makes the best *brigadeiros*. They're my favorite!"

Brigadeiros are Brazilian dessert balls. They are chocolate, chewy, and covered all over with chocolate sprinkles!

"Yummy," I say. I lick my lips.

I hope snack time is soon. But I have to finish my box first!

"Can I borrow your glue, please?" I ask.

"You bet," Ella says, passing it to me.

I squeeze another glob of glue onto my box.

Oops. I squeezed too much out by accident. I pour purple sparkles on top. *That's better!*

Margo turns toward my box.

"That is *not* a dot!" Margo scolds.

"Yes, it is. It's a *big* dot," I say.

She shoots her hand straight into the air. She is trying to tattle on me.

But Ms. Stoltz walks right past us to the front of the room. *Phew.* She rings the teacher's bell. *Ding. Ding.*

"It's time to clean up. Then, let's all find a carpet spot," Ms. Stoltz says. "I have exciting news to share with you all."

I make my ears real big. I smile big, too, so she knows I cannot wait to hear the exciting news.

Soon, Ms. Stoltz is counting down.

"Five . . . four . . . three . . . ," she begins. We are supposed to be sitting at a carpet spot by "zero."

I make it just in time. But Margo slides into my spot next to Ella!

"Hey!" I say.

"I saved that for Bessie," Ella says.

"Saving seats is against the rules," Margo says. She sits crisscross-applesauce.

"Bessie, Margo's right. Find another seat, please," Ms. Stoltz says.

Margo smiles. She sticks her chin up and flips her hair.

I squeeze in between Gorkem and Chris. Good thing I am teeny because there is not a lot of room.

"Hey, who's that?!" Chris asks.

He looks at a boy sitting between Ms.

Stoltz and Brayden. The boy has black hair,
like me. But I can't see his face. He is looking
down at his hands.

"Is he new?" Whitney asks. The whole class
is looking at the new boy next to her now. The
pretty beads in her braids jingle as she turns
to say, "Hi, I'm Whitney." Whitney is so nice.
She always smiles and says hi to everyone.

But the boy keeps looking down.

"Is he in our class for good?" Ella asks.

Ms. Stoltz puts her finger over her lips. This means we have to be quiet.

I use my fingers to "zip my lips," like Bailey always tells me to do.

Ms. Stoltz says, "I have two bits of exciting news! First, we have a new student. This is Jae

Jin Kwon. He would like us to call him Jae. Right?"

Ms. Stoltz turns to face the new boy. His head is still down. But he nods.

"Great!" says Ms. Stoltz. "We're so happy you're a part of our class! Friends, let's all make him feel welcome. Can we all say hi to Jae?"

"Hi, Jae," we all say together.

Jae gives a small wave. He still does not look up.

Maybe he is shy and scared. Just like me last year. I was new and had no friends yet.

"My second bit of news is about Valentine's Day," Ms. Stoltz says.

"YAY!" I shout. I cannot wait for Valentine's Day.

Ms. Stoltz smiles at me. She says, "Yes, Valentine's Day is only three days away. Our party on Monday is going to be extra special. We are going to give each other *secret* valentines this year."

Secret valentines? Ooh-la-laddie!

What is a secret valentine?!

2

A Special Task

At the carpet, Ms. Stoltz reads us a story. This one is about a grumpy bear and a gigantic box of chocolates and a secret valentine.

Margo sits tall and straight. She is still like a statue. Ella leans on her elbows, but she is being a good listener, too. I bounce-bounce-bounce in my seat. It is hard to sit still.

She reads a lot more pages. Finally, the story is over. Ms. Stoltz asks, "So, what makes a valentine special? What is a valentine *really* about?"

Margo raises her hand. She says a lot of things. But I am looking at Jae. He is not listening, either. He is picking the fuzz off the carpet. Why is he all the way in the back? Did he move when Ms. Stoltz started reading the story? *He looks so sad.*

I try to move back so I can say, *Hi! I'm Bessie! I'll be your friend.* I start to shuffle. But Ms. Stoltz stops me. She touches my knee.

She makes her lips go in a straight line. So I stay still.

Ms. Stoltz continues speaking. "For Valentine's Day this year, we are going to do something different. We will give class valentines AND one *special* valentine. Just like in the book. And you cannot tell anyone who your secret valentine is. We will not worry about who gave us what. We will focus on the message that we write to our secret valentine.

"You'll find out your secret valentine during Choice Time. I'll call you over one by one. Then, you'll pick a name out of a hat."

When it is Choice Time, we get to choose what activity we want to play.

Ella runs over to me.

"Whitney wants to play talent show again. You can show us a new magic trick! Want to join us?" Ella asks.

"I do!" I say. "But I want to play with Jae today. Next time!"

I walk super-duper fast to the Play-Doh center. I follow the rules. I *do not run.*

Gorkem, Brayden, Chris, and Jae are at the table already. And . . . so is Margo.

Everyone is playing with Play-Doh. But Jae is not. He's reading a big-kid book. It has no pictures! *He must be smart.*

"Hi! I'm Bessie!" I say.

Jae looks up at me. Then he looks back down at his book. He does *not* say hi back.

I plop down onto a chair. No one took the purple Play-Doh. Hooray! I grab it and smush it in my hands.

"He doesn't talk," Brayden says. He makes a pepperoni pizza out of red, orange, and yellow Play-Doh. Then he puts it over his face. "I am Pizza Man! I have cheese power!"

The boys and I giggle. Jae does not.

"That's gross," Margo says. "It's not supposed to go on your face." Brayden sticks his tongue out at Margo. But he takes the pizza off his face.

Margo rolls her eyes. She's hogging all the pink Play-Doh.

I try to talk to Jae again.

"Jae, what's your favorite color?" I ask. I shape my Play-Doh into a bunny, just like Baby Rabbit. Except Baby Rabbit is white and brown. Not purple.

Jae does not answer. He looks at Margo's pink Play-Doh. Then he hides his face in his book.

"He doesn't talk," Brayden says. "Remember?"

"I don't think he speaks English," Margo says. "Try another language."

"I speak Turkish!" Gorkem says. "*Merhaba*, Jae. *Merhaba* is hello."

Jae turns to Gorkem. He opens his mouth. But doesn't say anything. Then he hides his face in his book again.

"You try, Bessie," Margo says. "I bet you speak the same language."

"Why?" I ask.

"You know," Margo says, "because you look the same." She looks at me. And then at Jae.

"I thought he was in your family," she says. "You *really* look the same!"

I look at Jae. We do not look the same. Except for our hair color.

Jae still doesn't move.

"We do *not*," I say.

Chris looks at me and says, "I don't think you look the same."

"Me either," Brayden says.

"Me either," Gorkem says.

Jae still says nothing.

Margo shrugs her shoulders. "Where are you *really* from, anyway, Bessie?"

"Here!" I say. "Where are you from, Margo?" I ask.

"*Here*," Margo says. She rolls her eyes again.

"Stop, Margo," I say. I look right at her. I stand up. "You're being RUDE."

Margo's mouth hangs open. Her eyes get big. It looks like she might cry.

"*Sorry*," she whispers.

I shrug. "Okay," I say.

"Can I have some of your Play-Doh?" I ask. I plop back down. Margo slowly slides some to me.

Ms. Stoltz walks over. "Bessie, it's your turn," she says.

"MY SECRET VALENTINE!" I shout. *Finally!* I clean up my Play-Doh superfast.

"Are you ready to hear who you're

making a secret valentine for, Bessie?" she asks, once we arrive at her desk. I stand very still. I do not blink. I make my ears very, very big. And I nod my head seriously.

"Well," Ms. Stoltz starts. She shakes the black hat. It almost looks like my magician's hat! But not as fancy as mine. I dig my hands into it and pull a folded paper out of the hat.

"Let's see," Ms. Stoltz says. I give her the paper.

"Your secret valentine is . . . Jae!" Ms. Stoltz smiles. "Oh! You'll need to make it extra special. Make him feel welcome in our classroom. This is a very important job. Are you up for that, Bessie?"

"AM I EVER!" I shout. Then I cover my mouth. I remember that this is a *hush-hush* secret. "I will make the best secret valentine for Jae, Ms. Stoltz! It will make him feel

welcome!" I whisper-yell.

I jump up and down. This is not a teeny job at all. This is a big, special task.

I will make a secret valentine for the new kid.

It will be . . . magical!

3

A Sweet Trick!

When I get off the bus after school, Gramma waves to me.

She is wearing a dark purple shirt with lots of buttons. Her silver-and-black hair is curled extra fancy today.

I run and hug her. I wrap my legs around her like a koala. Hugging Gramma like this is fun!

"Gah Yee," Gramma says, calling my Chinese name. She chuckles as she sets me down. She cups my cheeks with her hands. It makes me warm all over, and I smile. Then, she points to the red minivan that she's standing in front of. Mom's car!

Gramma opens the car door and I jump inside.

"Mom! You're home early!" I say. I hug her even though she still has a seat belt on.

Mom's not wearing her lab coat. She always wears it when she works at the hospital.

"Where is your pharmer coat? Where's Daddy? Where's Bailey?" I ask.

Mom laughs. "I came home early because I had a dentist appointment. I don't need my *pharmacist* coat for that. Daddy is still at work. And Bailey's at her friend's house. She'll be back later," Mom says.

Boo. Bailey always has big-kid play dates. She says I'm too teeny to go with her.

But at least I get to go to the store! This means I get to pick the snacks I like!

"Can I bring Baby Rabbit?" I ask. I haven't seen Baby Rabbit in a million gazillion hours.

"No, Bessie. No pets at the store," Mom says.

"Pretty please?" I ask. "Pretty, pretty please?" I blink real slow so she knows I am being sweet.

Mom still says no. But she lets me run upstairs to say hi to Baby Rabbit before we go to the store.

I run to my room and give Baby Rabbit a big squeeze.

"Sorry I can't bring you to the store. But I have a surprise!" I say.

Baby Rabbit's ears perk up. I pull a bag of

carrots out of my pocket. It was extra from lunch. I saved them all day for Baby Rabbit.

Then I kiss Baby Rabbit on her soft head.

"I'll be back!" I say.

I grab my magic book and stuff it in my backpack.

At the Great Wall Supermarket, there are lots of yummy snacks. That's why I always want to go.

The words around the store are in Chinese and English. That's good for Gramma. She can't read English. Gramma says this store is the only place she can find the best vegetables for her soups.

Gramma loves the store more than me! She gets her own cart and zooms ahead to the vegetable section.

Other people try to get there, too. But Gramma gets right in front. She picks the greenest leafy stems. The other shoppers huff and wait. But Gramma keeps going. She bags bunches and bunches of them. Mom shakes her head. She says, "No one can get in the way of Gramma and her shopping."

"Go Gramma!" I cheer.

Mom lets me ride on the cart like a scooter. But she says I have to stay on the cart the whole time. Otherwise I run around too much. Mom

pushes the scooter while I ride.

I pretend the floor is lava!

"Faster, Mom! Before the lava sinks the scooter," I say.

"Is this a magic scooter?" Mom asks.

"Of course," I say.

When we pass things that I need, I put them in the cart. I have to be ready if lava covers the whole world! We will need lots of food. I grab cereal, Pocky sticks, and more cheesy doodles. Mom says no to only the cheesy doodles.

"We have a whole bunch at home," Mom says.

"Mom! The lava's coming! We need cheesy doodles," I say. I start to pout.

"Bessie . . . ," Mom says slowly. She makes her eyes big and her mouth tiny. That means I have to stop right now.

So I say, "Abracadabra-poof," my extra fancy magic word that makes magic appear. The lava turns back into the floor.

While Mom picks apples, I tell her all about my day at school. I tell her about my Valentine's Day box. And how I decorated it like a magician's box. I tell her about the new kid, Jae, too.

"Mom, why doesn't Jae talk?" I ask.

"He doesn't talk?" Mom asks.

I shake my head. "Not one bit," I say. "Is he scared?"

"Hmm. Maybe," Mom says. "Remember when you were the new kid in kindergarten? You were scared and shy, too. He'll open up when he's ready. Just make him feel welcome." Mom squeezes my hand.

"I will!" I say.

I tell her about the secret valentines. And my very important task.

Oh my! The secret valentine for Jae . . . I need to plan it. And it needs to be *extra special.* Magical.

The first part of planning a super-secret valentine is finding the perfect trick.

I pull out my magic book to get ideas. Then I crawl into the big part of the grocery cart. I have to scoot Mom's

groceries over to fit. Good thing I am teeny.

I tap-tap-tap my head. Maybe that will make some magic ideas appear into my mind. Nothing yet.

Gramma joins us again. Her cart is full of vegetables, meat, and oranges! My mouth waters at the oranges. Gramma buys them to give to our aunts and uncles. They always bring some to us, too. Gramma says oranges are good luck. Mom says it's nice to bring fruit to people's houses when you visit them. I like oranges because they're sweet.

That's it! My secret valentine should be sweet! And I know just the magic trick!

I find a folded-down page in my book that has sparkly star stickers on it. The magic trick on this page is called "Supersweet Secret." You need an orange and a secret note. The orange is closed. But when you open it up, there is a secret note inside!

Over winter break, Bailey helped me learn this trick. I performed it for my cousins, aunties, and uncles. Everyone loved it. I got a standing ovation. A *standing ovation* is when you are amazing. Everybody stands up and claps for you.

I will hide Jae's valentine inside an orange. It will be a hard magic trick. The biggest one I've done yet. And everyone will give him a standing ovation when he opens it. That will make him feel very welcome!

I look through the oranges in Gramma's cart. I spy one that is perfectly round. And big like a softball. It's just the orange I need for sticking a secret valentine inside.

Now I need to practice the trick.

And I know just the audience to practice on!

4

A Standing Ovation

Yummy!

I smell Gramma's dumplings. Most Saturdays, I run downstairs before everyone else wakes up and our relatives come to visit. Then I make dumplings and *jook*, or rice porridge, with Gramma. She lets me put as many salty peanuts as I want on top.

But today I need to practice my Supersweet Secret trick on my family. That way it will be perfect for Jae!

The first part of planning a super-secret valentine was finding the perfect trick. *Check.* The second part is preparing the trick. Good thing Gramma got a lot of oranges! I sneaky-snuck them into my room last night.

Ding dong!

Here comes my audience!

The door opens, and I hear my two uncles, three aunties, and four cousins happily greeting my parents.

I peek from my room.

"Hello! Hello! Come in!" Daddy says, opening the door. He's wearing his green golf shirt and holds a cup of coffee. It's still steaming. Mom is right beside him. Her arm is around Daddy's back. Aunt Sally, Aunt Lily, and Uncle Hank each hand Daddy a bag of oranges.

"Hey, guys!" Bailey calls from the kitchen.

Everyone takes off their shoes and puts on slippers. I wait until they shuffle into the kitchen. Now I hear lots of things. Dumplings sizzling. Everybody talking at the same time. And yelling. And laughing.

I smell so many things, too. Sweet dough-nuts. Scallion pancakes. Fried bread sticks to dip in the jook. My tummy grumbles.

Baby Rabbit jumps into my arms. She puts her front paws on my shoulders. She is ready to go downstairs, too. She is ready for our magic valentine trick.

"Not yet, Baby Rabbit," I say. "First, we have to be sneaky. We have to hide our valentines! Then we can do our performance."

I did not make valentines for my aunties, or uncles, or cousins. I do not want to make them sad by showing them the valentines I made. They would want one, for sure! That's why I need to hide the valentines for Bailey, Gramma, Mom, and Daddy in their rooms. They can find it later! And no one will be sad about not getting a valentine.

The valentines are not extra special. Not like the one I am making for Jae. But they still took me a million gazillion hours to make.

I used my best handwriting and drawing skills.

FOR MOM'S COIN COLLECTION

Dad says a "hole in one" is very good in golf!

SUPERGLUE! so the PENNY is Heads-up and lucky FOREVER!

After I put Gramma and Mom and Daddy's cards in their rooms, I sneak to Bailey's room. Baby Rabbit sniffs the door. I jiggle-jiggle-jiggle it. It's locked! She always locks me out of her room. Good thing I am magic. I can pick locks. Just like Houdini. I use my hairpin to poke the hole in the lock.

"Abracadabra-poof!" I say. I swing the door open.

Ooh-la-laddie. Bailey has lots of fun outfits. But I don't try them on today. I am *focusing*. I hang Bailey's valentine card on her ballet barre. I cut the card out like ballet slippers. And I used her real slippers to trace so that it is the right size. It's pink, her favorite color. I put sparkly stickers all over it. It's tied together with her favorite sparkly hair ribbon. I think it looks like real ballet shoes. Inside, I wrote:

On the way out, I see a bag of candy gummies. Yum! I only eat ten and give Baby Rabbit one. I do not want to spoil our appetite for dumplings and jook!

No one notices when I walk into the kitchen dressed as a magician. That's because I'm teeny. But then Uncle Hank says, "Hey! There she is!" He pats my magician's hat.

"Good morning!" Dad says. A toothpick wiggles from the corner of his mouth.

"Gah Yee," Gramma says, calling me over. She points to the empty chair at the little kid table. There's a bowl of jook and a plate of dumplings waiting for me.

"Where've you been, Teeny Houdini?" Bailey asks. She's sitting with the grown-ups. Even though she's just ten.

"Around," I say.

I sneaky-smile. Baby Rabbit jumps onto my lap.

"No pets while we're eating, Bessie," Mom says. "You know better."

"Okay," I say.

I hand Baby Rabbit a carrot from my pocket. She hops off and away.

Gramma adds a scallion pancake and a fried dough stick to my plate. I gobble up all my food.

Everyone talks at the same time. It is very loud. No one pays attention to me. So I go to the grown-up table. And I stand on an empty chair. It is time to practice my trick on an audience!

"*Ahem*," I say. This does not get their attention. I wave my magic cape. Glitter flies out onto the kitchen table.

"Bessie!" Bailey says. "I was still eating! Now there's glitter all over my jook! Ugh."

"Oops," I say. But I think her jook looks awesome now!

"I have a trick to perform. You will be my audience. Are you ready?" I ask.

Bailey glares at me. Even though she is the only one paying attention. So I look right at her and smile. Then, I say, again, "Are you ready?"

Bailey sighs. She picks the glitter out of her jook with her fingers. She says, "I'm *so* ready. I can *barely wait* . . ."

Yay! I give her the special orange.

"*I* showed you this trick, remember?" Bailey asks.

"Wait for the magic words," I say. "Then you can open it."

Bailey rolls her eyes. I tap the orange with my magic wand.

"*One. Two. Three.* Abracadra-poof!" I say. I wave my wand. I wiggle my cape. More glitter flies out.

"Are you *serious,* Bessie?!" Bailey yells. She looks down at all the new glitter in her jook. But then she opens the orange.

"What a surprise," she says, like a robot. "How on earth did that note get in there?"

I jump up and down. More glitter flies everywhere.

Bailey unrolls the secret note. "'Happy Valentine's Day, Jae!'" she reads. "Who's Jae?"

"He's my new friend," I say. "I'm going to

make him a secret valentine, like this."

"*Cool*," Bailey says. "Won't that be a big surprise?"

A *big* surprise?

Should I make a BIG surprise?

I look at all the glitter in Bailey's jook. She loved it!

Glitter. Glitter will make Jae's valentine more *magical*. But glitter won't fit into a normal orange. Unless . . . I make the orange big, big, big . . . then I can fill it with a note . . . *and* glitter. Ooh-la-laddie!

Just as I think it, Bailey stands up with her bowl of glitter jook to walk into the kitchen.

Hooray!

Every magician loves a standing ovation!

5

Make It Magical!

I grab two new bags of oranges and run upstairs to my room. None of the adults even saw me. They are busy talking in Chinese. And English. And laughing.

Baby Rabbit is on my bed, nibbling cheesy doodles. She has orange crumbs all over her whiskers.

"BABY RABBIT, IT WORKED! MY SUPERSWEET SECRET ORANGE TRICK WORKED!" I shout.

I plop the bags of oranges on the bed. They are heavy!

The next part of planning a super-secret valentine is to make it MAGICAL! It will be filled with glitter. The glitter will shoot out when Jae pulls the note out of the orange. It will shoot *everywhere*. Then Jae will get a standing ovation, too. But I will need to make this valentine big, big, bigger to fit the note and glitter. *A big surprise*, just like Bailey said.

I pull my notebook out from under my

pillow. I find more cheesy doodles hidden under the pillow, too. *Yum!*

I tap-tap-tap my head. I think. *What do I need to make this trick bigger?*

On my wall, there is a framed picture of me, Bailey, Mom, Daddy, and Gramma at Disney World. We are standing in front of a giant golf ball. Ooh-la-laddie! That gives me a good idea. I write down all the things I will need.

It is a good thing the grown-ups are busy talking. And playing mah-jongg. Mah-jongg is a game for grown-ups. They sit at a square table. And stack fancy, shiny blocks. And they throw the blocks in the middle of the table. There's a lot of noise. *Clink. Clang.* They shuffle the blocks. I tiptoe past them.

Bailey, cousin Lum Lum, and the other big kids are playing video games. All their eyes

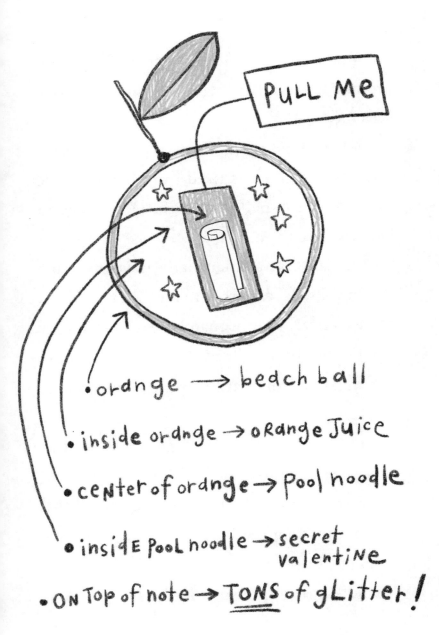

are glued to the TV. That means I can run around and gather materials. And no one sees me.

Whew. I am tired. That was a lot of materials. Baby Rabbit is tired from helping, too. She curls into a ball. And tucks in her paws to nap. I rub her head.

"You are a good magician's assistant, Baby Rabbit," I say. I carry her to my pillow so she is more comfy. I put the matching magician's hat I made her on her head. Next time I should not make it from cardboard. She just wants to eat it.

"Focus, Baby Rabbit," I say. "We need to supersize this valentine!"

First, I cut a little slit in the beach ball. All the air puffs out onto my face. I giggle.

Next, I need to fill it up with orange juice. Just like a real orange! I need a lot of orange juice. Good thing the aunties always bring oranges.

I squeeze, squeeze, squeeze. It is hard work! But I do not give up. Making something magical takes time. That's what Mom says.

Uh-oh.

I need a lot of tape.

And something to hold up my giant orange.

And something to cut the pool noodle.

And paint so it looks like an orange.

Wrapping paper! I cut a big piece. Then, I scribble "Happy Valentine's Day! From Your Secret Valentine" on the paper with a thick marker. It does not look so pretty. But that's okay. This is going to be the best valentine ever.

The giant orange takes a long time to make. I work. And work. And work. Baby Rabbit naps the whole time. It takes four big jars to fill the glitter to the top of the orange. *Will Jae like the magic I added to his valentine?* I jump up and down. I think he will! When I am finally done, I tap-tap-tap my wand on the side of the orange.

I say, "Abracadabra-poof!" Now it is a magic valentine!

That wakes Baby Rabbit up. She hops over to inspect the secret valentine. She twitches her nose. Her ears stick up.

"Isn't it special? It will be a big surprise!" I
say. Baby Rabbit just turns her head sideways.
Maybe she is still sleepy.

I plop onto my bed. I am all sticky. I'm
soaked, too. But at least I taste yummy. Baby
Rabbit thinks so. She licks the orange juice
off me.

Knock. Knock.

"Bessie, why's your door locked?" Mom
says through the door.

Uh-oh. My room is a big mess right now. Mom will be mad. I do not want to lie. So I tell a teeny truth. I say, "Baby Rabbit was napping."

"Oh, okay . . . Well, come on down, sweetheart. Gramma's got everything set up. We're going to make dumplings and rice cakes for the New Year."

Mom is talking about Lunar New Year. It's a special New Year we celebrate at the end of February. We make a lot of food for it. I love making food with the family. But I am still soaked from the orange juice.

"Uh . . . no, thank you," I say. I need to change super-duper fast.

My clothes are too sticky to take off. So I just put a shirt on top of the sticky one. And another. And another. I put on two pairs of pants. And a tutu. And a skirt. That's better!

"Come on, Bessie. You've been in here all afternoon. Goodness knows what you've been up to. We're making *dan tat*, too," Mom says.

"Dan tat?!" I yell. That's my favorite treat. "Why didn't you say so?!"

I swing my door open and run downstairs to get some dan tat!

6

The Night Before
Valentine's Day

After dinner on Sunday, Mom, Daddy, Bailey, Gramma, and I have lots to do! First, we go to the craft store. I get small blank cards to make valentines for my classmates. Then, Mom and Bailey need to go to the grocery store, again.

"Let's all stay together," Mom says.

Gramma shakes her head. She says she needs to go home to make soup.

"I need to go home, too. Please, please,

please!" I beg. "It's the night before Valentine's Day! I have a gazillion things to do!"

Mom sighs. They drop Daddy, Gramma, and me off at home.

Gramma winks at me on the way into our house. I giggle. Then she struts right to the stove to start making soup.

Daddy helps me make the valentines for all my classmates. He organizes all our stuff on the kitchen table. I pose Baby Rabbit *just right*. She sits on a pillow I shoved inside my upside-down magician's hat. I get my crayon ready to decorate the first card. On the outside, I am drawing Baby Rabbit popping out of a magician's hat. I write *Hoppy Valentine's Day!* The first card is for my friend Ella.

"How'd you come up with this clever line . . . *Hoppy Valentine's Day!?* It's funny," Dad says.

"Bailey helped me with the words. It was my idea to make the cards magic, though!" I say. I chose shiny silver paper for the inside of the cards. Daddy helps me cut the paper into stars. I write "You're a Star!" inside each card.

"These are pretty magical," Daddy says. He starts gluing the stars inside the cards.

"Of course!" I say. "But not as magical as my super-secret valentine for Jae! Do you think he'll like it, Daddy?"

"If it's made by you . . . he'll love it!" Daddy says. He pats my head with the part of his hand that's not gluey. I smile. *I hope Daddy's right!*

After we make cards for all my classmates and Ms. Stoltz, we let them dry on the kitchen table. Otherwise Daddy says they'll all stick together, like our fingers.

"Are we making the Valentine's Day party snacks now?"

"We're going to try!" Daddy says. He scratches his scruffy chin and squints at the recipe card.

We are going to make crispy-rice-cereal-marshmallow hearts! I spied the recipe on the back of the cereal box. It's perfect for the class party!

Daddy pours two whole bags of marshmallows and some butter into a large bowl.

He lets me sit on the counter so I can see them puff up in the microwave.

Gramma is near us at the stove. She's singing in Chinese and chopping vegetables for her soup. She's not paying any attention to us.

Next, Daddy lets me pour in the whole box of crispy rice cereal into the melted marshmallow and butter bowl.

"What's next, Daddy?" I ask. I lick some marshmallow off my fingers.

"Hmm . . . ," Daddy says. He scrunches his eyebrows.

"Oh, forget the recipe. How hard can this be?" he says. Daddy pushes the recipe card away.

"Let's stir it!" he says.

"Okay!" I say. I stick both arms into the bowl. *Aah*. It's gooey, warm, and supersticky.

"Bessie!" Daddy yells. "Not with your

hands. That's what a spoon is for!"

Oh. Daddy is right. This was not a good idea.

The melted marshmallow and crispy-rice-cereal mixture is stuck to my arms. There is nothing left in the bowl.

"Phooey!" I say. I cross my arms and pout.

"No!" Daddy yells.

Now the marshmallow and crispy-rice-cereal mixture is stuck to my shirt, too. Plus, my arms are stuck together. For real.

I try to move my arms. My arms are buried inside the dried marshmallows. I am going to be a marshmallow-crispy-rice-cereal statue forever. And I ruined my special Valentine's Day snack.

"Daddy!" I cry. I stomp my feet. It's all I can move!

Daddy laughs. Then he covers his mouth.

"Sorry," he says. He hugs me. "Oh, *Bessie*. What do I even do about this?"

"*Ma, bong sow,*" Daddy calls to Gramma. That means, "Mom, help," in Chinese.

Gramma turns around fast. She has ginger in one hand and spring onions in the other. When she sees me looking like a marshmallow-rice-crispy statue, she laughs, too.

"Hey!" I say. But then I think how funny it is . . . and I start to laugh also.

Daddy and Gramma clean me up. We have to throw away the marshmallow-crispy-rice-cereal snack. But I save a teeny bit to give to Baby Rabbit.

Good thing Gramma made lots of my favorite mini egg pie desserts, dan tats, yesterday.

There is enough to bring in for my Valentine's Day party snack. Daddy, Gramma, and I decorate the dan tats.

We laugh and laugh the whole time. We keep remembering how I was stuck as a marshmallow-rice-crispy statue. These extrafancy dan tats are better than marshmallow-rice-crispy hearts, anyway.

I squeeze a sparkly red icing heart on top of the last dan tat. TA-DA!

I'm finally ready for my Valentine's Day party!

7

The Valentine's Day Party

When I wake up Monday morning, it's still dark! I'm too excited to wait for my alarm clock. Or the sunlight.

"BABY RABBIT, IT'S VALENTINE'S DAY!" I shout.

She does not wake up. I pat-pat-pat her head.

"Baby Rabbit? Wake up," I say.

Baby Rabbit turns around. Her fluffy butt faces me.

"Okay, okay," I whisper gently.

I get dressed all by myself. I can't choose what shirt to wear. Should I wear a red one with a big sparkly silver heart? *Perfect for Valentine's Day.* Or a purple one with magic silver stars? *Perfect for a magician.* I can't decide, so I put on both. Then I find my puffy pink vest. It's soft and pink for Valentine's Day, too. I choose my red tutu. And pink leggings. Plus one striped sock. And one cheetah-print sock. The cheetah spots kind of look like hearts! Ooh-la-laddie. *I look fancy.*

Knock. Knock.

"Bessie, what's going on in here?" Daddy asks. He's wearing his flannel pajamas. And his hair is all stuck to one side of his head.

"It's too early. What's all that noise?" he asks. He rubs his eye.

"I got dressed all by myself!" I say.

Daddy looks at my open drawers with all the clothes falling out.

"Wow . . . ," he says. Daddy laughs. He shakes his head.

"Is it time for my Valentine's Day party yet?" I ask. I jump up and down.

"Soon, darling . . . soon. I've got to get ready for court now," he says. Then he kisses my hair.

I also have to go get ready . . . for school! I carefully put my Valentine's Day cards into my backpack. Then I peek inside the tin tray full of dan tats for the Valentine's Day party. They smell yummy and look fancy!

I stick my super-secret valentine in a big brown box. I found the box in Mom and Daddy's room. It's the perfect size to hide Jae's valentine in. It is super-duper big and heavy. Gramma helps me carry it to the bus.

Then, Ms. Alrahhal sees Gramma carrying the big box. She makes her big-kid son carry it instead.

"Thank you!" I say.

Ms. Alrahhal nods. She elbows her son.

He half smiles. "No problem," he says.

He even helps me carry it off the bus. Our bus driver, Ms. Pat, calls him a gentleman. That makes him smile real big. Then he helps me carry the secret valentine into my classroom before saying goodbye.

I am the first one here! I even beat Ms. Stoltz.

The whole classroom looks different today. Beautiful and magical. Across the chalkboard is a gold-and-red "HAPPY VALENTINE'S DAY!" banner. There are pink and red twisted streamers dangling from the ceiling. Shiny red hearts hang down over each of our desks, too. Ms. Stoltz put up our "What Is Love?" art projects on the bulletin board. And the big tables are covered with pink and red tablecloths. Ooh-la-laddie! I cannot wait for our party.

Thud. Thump. Thud. Thump. My class-mates are coming! I walk super-duper fast out of the classroom. I'm first in line outside the door. Ella pops up right behind me.

"Hi, Bessie!" Ella says. "Look what I'm wearing!" She unzips her coat with one hand to show me her shirt. It's turquoise with a big silver heart on it.

"Run your hand across it!" she says.

I move my hand over the heart. The silver sequins turn red. *How magical!*

"Ooh! Look at mine!" I have to put my tray of snacks down in the hallway because my arms are too teeny. Then, I unzip my puffy vest and hold out my star shirt. I show Ella my heart shirt, too!

"It doesn't change colors like yours. But it's a heart for Valentine's Day!" I say.

"It's awesome!" Ella says. "What'd you

bring for the snack? I brought brigadeiros."

"Yes!" I cheer. "I brought dan tats." I lift the cover to show her the hearts I decorated on top.

"Yum! I can't wait," Ella says.

Click. Clack. Click. Clack. Ms. Stoltz walks past us. She's wearing a red knit sweater with a gold heart pinned on the front. Her earrings are big, clip-on hearts with smiley faces on them.

"Good morning, girls!" she says. "How festive you both look!"

"Good morning, Ms. Stoltz!" Ella and I respond.

She directs us into the classroom.

"You can put your snacks on the table with the pink tablecloth. We'll save those for the party. After you unpack, you can put your Valentine's Day box on your desk. We'll hand out the class valentines first thing this morning. We'll save the secret valentines for the party!" Ms. Stoltz says.

Ella grabs my hands. We jump up and down. I cannot wait for the Valentine's Day party! I cannot wait for Jae to open my super-secret magical valentine!

I bring my fancy magician valentine box to my desk. After Ms. Stoltz takes attendance, we take turns walking around and dropping our everybody valentines into one another's boxes. *Will my classmates like my magic Valentine's Day cards? Will Jae?*

I shake my magician valentine's box to feel how many cards and treats are inside. It's heavy! The rainbow glitter on my box sparkles in the light. I smile. This is going to be the most magical Valentine's Day!

Ding. Ding. Ding. Ding.

Ms. Stoltz has to ring the bell a million gazillion times all morning. Because we all have so much *energy*. That means that no one is listening very good. Not even Margo. Everyone keeps getting up when it's not their turn. And asking if it's time for the Valentine's Day party yet. And walking over to see Jae's very big secret valentine. They try to guess who gave it to him. Even though we're not supposed to. Even though I want to say, *It's me! It's me! I made the magical super-big secret valentine for Jae!* I do not. Because I promised Ms. Stoltz I wouldn't.

Jae is the only one still sitting down. I think he is smiling. But I cannot tell, because he covered his mouth with his hand all morning. I can't wait for him to open the valentine. Then he'll be happy, for sure!

Ding.

"Guess what it's time for, friends?" Ms. Stoltz says.

"THE VALENTINE'S DAY PARTY!" I scream. I am so excited that I forget all the rules. I tug-tug-tug on Ms. Stoltz's sweater. I stand super-duper close to her. She laughs.

"Yes, it's time for our Valentine's Day party! First, we'll play a game. Then, we'll open our secret valentines. When I ring the bell, you may walk *slowly* to the carpet."

Ding.

Everyone runs.

8

Soaked

Ms. Stoltz teaches us how to play Musical Hearts.

"Hearts are laid around the edge of the carpet. You will start by standing behind a heart. When I play the music, you will walk around the carpet until the music stops. Once the music stops, you want to be standing in front of a heart. Look at the dance move on the heart. Copy it! But every round, I will take a heart away. If you don't have a heart to stand in front of, you're out of the game and can come sit in the middle of the carpet. We'll play until we have one winner. Are you all ready?" asks Ms. Stoltz.

"Yeah!" we all say. Ella and I smile real big at each other.

"I bet you'll be good at this," I say to her. "Because you're so good at Hula-Hooping."

"Maybe!" she says.

Everyone stands in front of a heart. Then Ms. Stoltz plays the first song.

We all walk super-duper slow. Because no one wants to be out.

Gorkem doesn't walk at all. So Brayden runs into him. I run into him. And Ella runs into me. Then Margo runs into her.

"Hey!" Margo calls. "The rules are that you have to keep moving."

"IT'S NOT ME!" Brayden shouts.

"Gorkem stopped walking," Ella says.

I don't say anything. Because my face is smushed into the back of Brayden's shirt.

Ms. Stoltz stops the music.

"Gorkem, you have to keep moving. See what happens when you don't?" she says.

"Okay," Gorkem says. "But I don't want to get out."

"Everyone will get out at some point," Ms. Stoltz says. "Except our winner. But that's okay. We're all going to have fun with it! Ready to try again?"

"Ready," I hear everyone say. Even though it sounds muffled.

"Where's Bessie?" Ms. Stoltz asks.

"Oh, here!" Ella says. She backs up. Then I back up. "Oops," she says.

Whew, I sigh. It feels good to not be smushed.

Everyone laughs. Because I am so funny.

Ms. Stoltz starts the music, again. This time, we all walk. When the music stops, I look down. There's a heart. Yay! I'm still in. My heart has a picture of a chicken on it. I don't know what the chicken dance is. I just act like a chicken. I flap my hands. I turn in circles. I stick my neck out. And say, "Bawk! Bawk! Bawk!"

Everyone has a different dance. We are all having fun. Even Chris, who's sitting in the middle of the carpet. He got out.

When the music stops the next time, I land on the heart with a picture of Rufus on it! Rufus is our class pet hamster.

"Rufus! Rufus! Look, it's you!" I say. Rufus stops eating. He lifts his front paws and looks at me. I pretend I am running in a hamster wheel. I crouch down. And move my hands and feet really fast. And twitch my nose like Rufus.

"Bessie, that's so good!" Ella says. She falls to the floor laughing. I do it some more.

Then, Ella rolls over on her back. She kicks her hands and feet up in the air. Her heart has a picture of a beetle on it.

Margo flaps her wings like a butterfly. She looks so elegant!

Gorkem does the "Floss" dance.

Brayden hops on one foot.

Whitney waves her hands up at the same time. Then she pretends she's eating an invisible pizza.

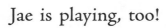

Jae is playing, too!

He squiggles like a worm on the floor. But he won't look up. He just looks at the floor.

"Ms. Stoltz is playing, too," Ella says. She points to Ms. Stoltz. We all stop dancing and look. Ms. Stoltz moves her arms and head slowly. Like a robot. It is so funny. We all laugh out loud.

We play round. After round. After round.

It is a good thing I wore so many layers. Because I get so hot from dancing. I take off lots of stuff. But I still have on two shirts. And my vest. That's better!

Now there are only three of us still standing. It is me and Margo and Jae.

"I am going to try my best!" I say. "But I hope *you* win, Jae."

Jae doesn't say anything. But his face turns red like a tomato.

Margo rolls her eyes. "I'm the best dancer here," she says.

"Maybe," I say back.

"I hope you win," Jae whispers to me.

He talked!

My mouth hangs open.

Jae smiles. Then, he covers his mouth real fast. But I think I hear him giggle.

Ms. Stoltz plays the music. Margo, Jae, and I start walking. I can't go as fast because my legs are teeny. But I try to keep up. When the music stops, I look down. There's a heart! Jae is standing in front of a heart, too. That means . . .

Margo is out! Margo puts her hands on her hips.

"I wanted to be out, anyway. This isn't *real* dancing," she says. She struts to the middle of the carpet.

My heart has a picture of a bunny on it.

I hop-hop-hop just like Baby Rabbit. And wiggle my invisible tail.

"What's Jae's dance?" Brayden asks.

"Ooh, maybe he's a statue!" Ella says.

"Maybe he's frozen," Whitney says.

I look down at his heart. It has a bear on it. But Jae does not dance like a bear. He does not dance at all. He just looks frozen. *What is he staring at?*

I follow Jae's eyes.

He is staring at his desk.

Uh-oh.

The super-duper magical secret valentine on his desk is NOT super-duper big anymore.

The giant orange ball is now flat. There is orange juice *everywhere*. It's dripping down the sides of Jae's desk. And all over his seat. And all over the floor.

Everything on the desk is soggy. So soaked. Totally, completely *ruined*.

My eyes almost pop out. I slap my hands to my face.

I turn to look at Jae.

He does not say anything. He does not move. He does not blink. But one teeny tear drops out of his eye . . . and falls down his face.

Mayhem

Everyone crowds around Jae's desk.

Drip. Drip. Drip.

There's orange juice all over the desk and trickling onto the floor. It's everywhere.

"What a mess!" Margo says. "Who would make such a ridiculous Valentine, anyway? Now everything's ruined."

She turns to look straight at me. And lifts an eyebrow.

I look away.

Jae's still standing at the carpet. He's a sad statue.

I want to cry.

"Oh no," Ella says. "All his valentines are ruined."

"Especially his secret valentine," Margo says. She points to the orange paint glob sliding off the beach ball.

I want to run away. And hide in my cubby. But then everyone will know it was me. *And that it's all my fault.*

"Okay, okay," Ms. Stoltz says. She walks over to us. "We're going to take a movement break outside. We'll continue the party in a bit. Please walk around the mess. Line up at the door. A teacher will meet you in the hallway."

Everyone starts to move.

Ms. Stoltz walks over to me. She whispers, "Stay behind, please."

I'm in *big* trouble.

Ella turns to me as she gets in line. "Are you coming?" she asks.

I shake my head.

"*Oh*," she says.

If I look at Ella, I will cry, for sure. I turn my face away. But instead I just see Margo giving me a weird look. *Ugh.*

The door closes. Everyone is out of the classroom. Except for me and Ms. Stoltz. She kneels down to my height. I feel extrateeny right now.

"How did this happen, Bessie?" she asks.

"I . . . I . . ." I try to tell Ms. Stoltz. But I cannot. Big tears make water balls in my eyes.

"Oh, sweetie," Ms. Stoltz says. She sits down on the floor. She rubs my back.

I cry. And cry. And cry. It feels good to let it out. And I cannot stop. *I ruined Jae's secret valentine. I ruined everything.*

We sit together for a long time before I can calm down. Finally, I say, "Ms. Stoltz, I made a bad valentine." I hide my face in a crumpled tissue.

"Hmm," Ms. Stoltz says. "What do you think makes a *good* valentine?"

"One that is big, big, big!" I say. "Like in the book you read. And one that is magic. It gives someone a standing ovation! That's what I wanted to do, Ms. Stoltz. I wanted to give Jae a big standing ovation. So he knows he is welcome. But then—" I can't finish my words.

I still hear the *drip-drip-drip* coming from Jae's desk.

"Well," Ms. Stoltz begins. She hands me another tissue. I blow my nose loudly.

"Better?" Ms. Stoltz asks. She smiles.

I nod.

"Bessie, in the book, the valentine wasn't

special because it was big. It was special because it made Mr. Bear feel loved and welcome. How do you think Jae is feeling as the new kid? How can you *really* make him feel welcome?"

"I don't know," I say softly. *Because I ruined everything.*

"Of course you do, Bessie. You'll think of something. You're magic, remember? I know you can do it," she says. She winks at me.

"Now, about this mayhem . . . ," Ms. Stoltz says. She looks over at Jae's desk.

"I'll clean it," I say. I pop up off the floor. I grab a million gazillion paper towels to clean up my big, big, big mess. Because I am responsible!

It takes a long time to wipe everything down. I hear everyone running and having fun outside. But I bet Jae is not having fun.

I wonder if he's still crying. Thinking about what happened makes my heart feel squishy.

I throw away the last of the soggy Valentine's Day cards.

Wait! I have an idea. I will give him *my* class valentine cards. And I will make him a new box, too.

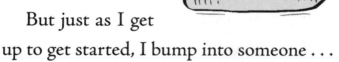

But just as I get up to get started, I bump into someone . . .

"Margo? What are you doing here?" I ask. I am too scared to hear her say, *I know it was you.*

"I . . . came to help you," Margo says. Her eyes are wet. She gives me a small smile. "I think your giant valentine was really cool, Bessie. Sorry I made you sad," she says.

"Oh," I say. "Thank you, Margo. Want to help me make a new Valentine's Day box for Jae?"

"Sure," Margo says. "I'm really good at making Valentine's Day boxes. What color should we make it?"

"I think I know," I say.

I grab some pink construction paper.

10

A Big Heart

After school, I still feel bad. *Because I ruined the Valentine's Day party.* And I *did not* make Jae feel welcome. I made Jae *cry*.

I let Gramma carry me back from the bus stop. I am cold. And sad. And tired.

Gramma is warm and cozy. Hugging Gramma always makes me feel better.

I kiss her cheek.

When we get inside, I run right to my room.

Baby Rabbit is already sitting on my bed.

"How'd you get out of your cage?" I ask.

I pull out a lollipop from my pocket. It's the only treat I saved from the class valentine cards. I put the rest in Jae's new valentine box. I scoop Baby Rabbit up and squeeze her.

That's when I see what Baby Rabbit was sitting on.

"Ooh-la-laddie!" I say.

There is a present on my bed. It has a bow tied around it. And a little note that says:

Happy Valentine's Day, Teeny Houdini!
I hope it's as magical as you are!

Love,
Bailey

I jump up and down. I love presents. I carefully tear open the wrapping paper. There is a shiny, sparkly silver star patch inside. It's the size of my hand. WOW!

"IT'S MAGICAL!" I shout.

I run my fingers carefully over the patch. Then I grab my purple magician's cape off my nightstand. The star patch is perfect for it!

Bailey walks into my room.

"So you like my valentine, huh?" Bailey asks.

"I love it, Bailey!" I say. "Can you help me put it on my cape?"

"What do you think I brought an iron for?" Bailey asks. She plugs the iron into the wall socket. "Stand back, okay?"

I take a teensy step back. While Bailey irons the star patch onto my cape, I lick the lollipop from my pocket.

Then I give Baby Rabbit a few licks.

"Want a lick?" I ask. I hold the lollipop out to Bailey.

"Umm . . . pass," Bailey says. "I'm glad you love the star patch. I saved some babysitting money to buy it. Found the most magical one," she says. "I really loved the card you made me, Bessie. That was really sweet."

"That was teeny," I say. "Not special like this." I wrap the magician cape all around me. The star patch is still warm from the iron. It shines and sparkles!

I take another lick of the lollipop.

"Oh my goodness . . . ," Bailey says. "It's all over your face, Teeny." She brings over a wet towel. "Come here. Ugh, *gross*." She wipes my face softly.

"Want to do a puzzle together?" Bailey asks.

"You don't have dance practice?" I ask.

"Not today," she says.

"You want to play . . . with *me*?!" I ask. I jump up and down.

"Well . . . ," Bailey says. "I want to spend Valentine's Day with my little sis. Even if you're a big pain most of the time!"

"HOORAY!" I shout. Bailey rolls her eyes, but smiles.

Baby Rabbit is happy, too. She hops onto my shoulder. And licks more of the lollipop.

Bailey pours the puzzle onto the carpet. Good thing I cleaned this morning. Or we would not have anywhere to play!

It is a rabbit puzzle with a picture of a mommy rabbit and her bunnies. Baby Rabbit *loves* this puzzle.

Bailey hands me the edge pieces. I fit them together. I am so fast. I puzzle. And lick my lollipop. Puzzle and lick. Puzzle and lick. My magic cape with my superspecial star patch stays wrapped around me.

Bailey works in the middle of the puzzle. She is so *smart*. And super at puzzles.

Then Bailey takes some of the pieces I put together. And puts them in a new place.

"How'd your big secret valentine surprise go?" she asks.

I freeze. Tears come back to my eyes.

"It was a big mess . . . ," I whisper. "It wasn't magical *at all*."

"Oh." She is quiet for a little bit. Then she says, "Why don't you make him something else?"

"Like the card you made me," Bailey says. "It was small. But superspecial. You wrote a sweet note. And I like how you made it shaped like ballet shoes."

"Like the star patch you got me because I'm a magician!" I say. I push a puzzle piece into another one. Bailey takes it out. And fits it in the right place, for real.

"Yeah! It was really thoughtful," Bailey says.

"What's *thoughtful*?" I ask. I lay the lollipop on the carpet. And let Baby Rabbit lick the rest. I am too sticky now.

"Yuck . . . ," Bailey says, looking at the lollipop. "*Thoughtful* is when you think about what someone else wants or needs. Like . . . this kid is new, right?"

"Yeah," I say.

I pick the lollipop off the carpet and put it on my bed. So it will not be yucky.

"So pretend you're the new kid. What's he like? What would he want? You don't need big *magic*, Teeny Houdini. Use your big *heart*," Bailey says.

"Hmm," I say. I think about how much I love my star patch. *What would Jae like?* I pull my magic wand out of my cape and tap-tap-tap my brain to remember all the things I've seen him do.

"You are so smart, Bailey!" I say. She smiles.

Bailey hands me the last puzzle piece to put in. TA-DA! We finished the puzzle. Perfect timing, too. Because now I have a new super-secret valentine to make.

And I know just what kind of magic it needs!

11

A Magical Friendship

The next day, I'm first in line to walk into our classroom. I can't wait to give Jae his new secret valentine!

After I say good morning to Ms. Stoltz, I race over to Jae's seat. The new pink valentine box that Margo helped me make is on the desk already. All the valentine cards from my box are inside. But Margo and I changed the names on the cards to Jae's. Now the cards are all for him!

I slide the secret valentine onto his super-clean desk. Then I head over to the cubbies, so no one knows it was from me.

Our warm-up today is a heart coloring page. But I cannot focus on coloring because I keep staring at the door. I'm waiting for Jae to walk in. But he doesn't.

Ms. Stoltz takes attendance after the morning bell rings. When she calls Jae's name, no one answers.

I look over at his chair . . . it's empty. Where is he? How can I give him his secret valentine if he's not here?

Maybe he is sad because all his valentines were ruined.

And he did not get a secret valentine. And now he hates our class. And never wants to come back. All because of me.

I raise my hand.

"Yes, Bessie?" Ms. Stoltz asks.

"Where is Jae?" I ask.

"Oh, he's not here. I'm sure he'll be back tomorrow," she says. She smiles at me.

"He has to come back," Margo says. "He has a new valentine's box. It's even better than the first one. Right, Bessie?" She smiles and flips her hair.

She doesn't wait for me to answer. She goes back to coloring her warm-up. She colors right in the lines. And doesn't leave any white spots.

I can't answer her, anyway. If I say anything, I will cry.

I walk over to Jae's seat. *Why isn't he here?* I walk in circles around his desk.

Margo raises her hand to tattle on me. But I don't care.

I close my eyes and say the magic words over and over again.

"Abracadabra-poof. Abracadabra-poof. Abracadabra-poof," I say. I hope Jae will magically appear.

It works!

Jae walks through the door with his head down. I scramble back to my seat. I pretend not to stare at him. He hands Ms. Stoltz a note.

"Oh, you were with our reading teacher for the new-student testing!" Ms. Stoltz says. "She says you did a wonderful job, Jae!"

Jae gives Ms. Stoltz a little smile.

Then he unpacks for a million gazillion minutes. Finally, he goes to his desk.

Jae runs his hands over his new pink Valentine's Day box. He lifts the lid to peek inside.

I can't see his face. *Is he smiling? Is he happy?* Finally, he picks up the secret valentine.

I remember Ms. Stoltz said we are not supposed to say who our valentine is. So I pull a book out from my desk. I stand it up so it blocks my face. Now I can sneaky-peek at Jae opening his secret valentine.

He buries his head in the card as he reads it.

Dear Jae,

Welcome to our class. You are new, but there are lots of nice friends in here. I would love to be your friend. Do you like the pink card? Do you like your pink Valentine's box and the new Valentine's cards? I think you like pink because you were looking at Margo's pink Play-Doh. Also, you have a turtle key chain on your backpack. So I drew turtles for you.

Also, do you like Pocky sticks? You ate the chocolate ones on Friday. I can share my strawberry ones with you. I hope you have a good day. If you want to play with me, I will be at the red table at Choice Time. I really want to be your friend.

Love,
      Your Secret Valentine

Even though I can't see, I know what it says. And I know it has perfect spelling. Because Bailey helped me with the hard words.

Jae looks at the card for a long time. Then he shoves it in his pocket. He covers his face with his arm. And pulls his coloring page close to him. I can't see anything.

After a gazillion bajillion hours, it is finally Choice Time. I wait at the red table. I sit on my favorite yellow ball chair. But I am too worried to bounce.

Will Jae come?

I breathe so loud I can hear myself. Jae is still sitting at his desk. He does not look at me. He does not walk to the red table.

I sigh.

I open the box of dominoes. One by one, I stand them up. I will make a big heart.

Just as I put down a domino, I feel a tap on my shoulder.

"Can I play?" someone asks.

I turn around.

It's Jae!

"Yeah," I say. I smile.

He sits down.

"Thanks for being so nice to me. I didn't know you knew all that about me. How do you know so much?" Jae asks.

"I don't know," I say. I think more about his question. Then I say, "I just saw you! I kept looking with my magician's eye."

"I like your fancy cape!"

I scoot the last pile of dominoes over to him.

We take turns placing dominoes to make the domino heart. When we finish, I ask, "What should we knock down?"

I point to the last domino. It's at the bottom of the heart.

"Let's try this," Jae says. He adds an empty gallon container to the lineup.

"Awesome!" I say. "Okay. Ready, set . . ."

"GO!" Jae shouts. He taps the first domino. Off they go!

When the last domino hits the gallon container, it goes flying. It accidentally bounces off Margo's head.

Jae and I burst out laughing.

Ms. Stoltz walks over.

"That's a big heart for a teeny girl," Ms. Stoltz says.

"Yeah, it is," I say.

"I knew I could count on you," Ms. Stoltz says. She looks at Jae. And then winks at me.

Jae and I are still laughing. It's funny that a small thing can make something big happen. Just like dominoes. Or a little secret valentine.

Jae sets up the dominoes again.

"Wait," I say. "This time, let's do it with magic."

I grab my magic wand from my backpack.

And a bag full of rainbow glitter.

After all, everything's better with a teeny bit of magic!